PHOEBE'S PARADE

by **Claudia Mills**

illustrated by **Carolyn Ewing**

Macmillan Publishing Company New York *Maxwell Macmillan Canada* Toronto

Maxwell Macmillan International New York Oxford Singapore Sydney

Library of Congress Cataloging-in-Publication Data. Mills, Claudia. Phoebe's parade / Claudia Mills ; illustrated by Carolyn Ewing. — 1st ed.   p.   cm. Summary: Not even her brothers' teasing can spoil Phoebe's excitement about being a Peewee Majorette in the Fourth of July parade.   ISBN 0-02-767012-0 [1. Parades—Fiction. 2. Drum majorettes—Fiction. 3. Brothers and sisters—Fiction.] I. Ewing, C. S., ill. II. Title. PZ7M63963Ph 1994   [E]—dc20   93-21861

E
FIC
Mills
Claudia

For Jillian Hershberger and all the children
of Takoma Park, Maryland—C. M.

To John—C. W.

It was the Fourth of July, and Phoebe was going to be in the parade. Not her brother David. Not her brother Carter. Just Phoebe.

As soon as she woke up, Phoebe leaped out of bed, tore off her nightgown, and put on her leotard. It was red, with shiny blue and white stars all over it. The stars were made of tiny sequins that caught the light and sparkled.

Phoebe ran outside in her bare feet. She didn't want the wet grass to touch her new white sandals.

Across the street, Mr. Harsanyi was hanging out his flag.

"Guess what?" Phoebe called to him. "I'm going to be in the parade. With the Peewee Majorettes. I'm going to carry a baton!"

"That's great, Phoebe," Mr. Harsanyi said.

Next door, Mrs. Steinhart was outside with her dog.

"I'm going to be in the parade," Phoebe told her. "Not Carter or David. Only me."

"I'll be watching for you," Mrs. Steinhart said.

David and Carter were helping Daddy take their new flag out of its cardboard box.

"Today's my parade!" Phoebe told them, as if they didn't already know.

"Big deal," said Phoebe's older brother, David.

But Carter, who was only four, looked wistful. "I want to be in the parade, too," he said.

"Everyone can't be in the parade," Phoebe explained to him kindly. "But at least you can watch me and cheer when I go by."

David put his arm around Carter. "Carter and I just want to see the fire engines. Right, Carter?"

"Right," Carter echoed. Then he asked Phoebe, "Can I hold your baton?"

"No," Phoebe said.

"For one minute? I'll be real careful."

Phoebe shook her head. "You have to hold it right, or you might drop it," she said.

"Give me a break," David said. "You're not even throwing it up in the air. You're just carrying it, like a dumb old stick."

"*You're* a dumb old stick," Phoebe said.

"Hey, I thought of a tongue twister," David said. "Try to say this three times fast: Braggy Peewee Phoebe, Braggy Peewee Phoebe, Braggy Peewee Phoebe."

"Children!" Mommy said, coming outside to admire the flag. "Let's not have any squabbling."

Breakfast took forever. Finally Daddy loaded the folding chairs into the station wagon. Mommy gave David and Carter each a small flag of their own, to wave at Phoebe when she marched by. But the boys jabbed each other with them instead.

Daddy dropped Phoebe off at the beginning of the parade route.

"You're the first one here, Phoebe," said Mrs. Evans, the parade lady.

While she waited, Phoebe practiced holding her baton. Then she tried throwing it up into the air, the way the big girls did. She almost caught it.

She tried again, tossing it higher this time. Another miss.

Then she tried once more, not as high, and caught it!

The five other Peewees arrived, and the five big girls who were the real majorettes, and finally the head majorette, Marie. When Marie tossed her baton into the air, it went higher than the telephone wires, and she caught it every time.

"Let's line up," Mrs. Evans said. "We're right before the high school marching band and the fire engines."

Phoebe took her place, her heart pounding with excitement.

The parade began!

First came the antique cars carrying the mayor and the city council. Behind them came the America the Beautiful float. Then the drum and fife corps. Then the world peace and brotherhood float. Then Marie and the big girl majorettes.

And then, Phoebe! Phoebe and all the other Peewee Majorettes.

Phoebe stood as straight as her baton. She felt as sparkly as the sequins on her leotard.

After a few blocks, Phoebe was hot. The back of her neck was sweaty, and her feet in her new sandals began to hurt. But she didn't care.

In the crowd Phoebe saw Mr. Harsanyi. He waved at her. Mrs. Steinhart waved at her, too.

Step, step, step, step.

At last, a few blocks later, Phoebe saw Daddy and Mommy and David and Carter. Phoebe put on her best parade face for Daddy's pictures.

Ahead of her, Marie tossed her baton high into the air and caught it, one-handed, without missing a beat. The crowd cheered.

Suddenly, Phoebe hurled her own baton into the air. How the crowd would cheer when *she* caught it! David and Carter wouldn't dare tease her about anything ever again.

But Phoebe didn't catch her baton. Instead of returning to her waiting hands, the baton soared over the heads of the crowd and landed out of sight.

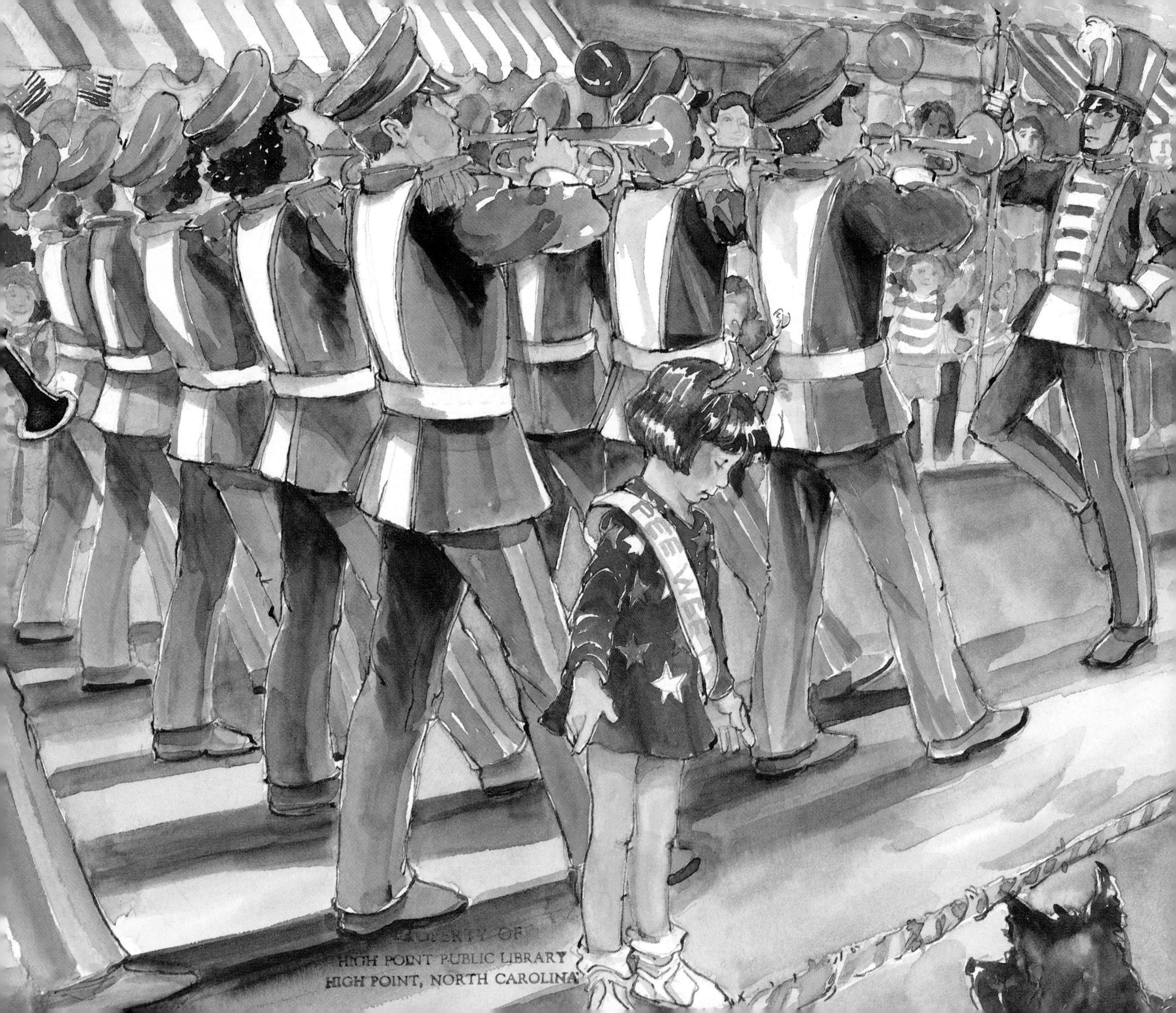
PEE WEE

Phoebe froze in place. The high school band marched past her as she stood all alone by the side of the parade route, stiff with shame. People were laughing. People were laughing at *her*, at Braggy Peewee Phoebe. Her brothers would tease her about this for the rest of her life.

But when she made herself look at them, they weren't laughing, not even David, though Phoebe could tell he was trying hard not to.

"Here." David handed Phoebe her baton. "Carter found it for you."

Phoebe didn't want her baton, but she took it. She hated her baton now. She hated everything about the Fourth of July.

The first of the fire engines was coming right behind her. Phoebe stepped aside miserably to let it go by.

"Hey, little girl, want a ride?" One of the fire fighters grinned down at her.

Phoebe could hardly believe her ears. All at once life was wonderful again.

"Yes," she whispered, wiping her eyes.

The fire engine stopped, and the fire fighter helped Phoebe climb on.

Riding on a real fire engine was even better than being a Peewee Majorette. Below her, Phoebe saw Daddy snapping pictures. She saw David and Carter, their faces filled with longing.

Phoebe thought fast.

"Please," she said to her fire fighter, "can my brothers have a ride, too?"

"Sure," he said.

A different fire fighter reached out a hand to David and Carter, and they scrambled aboard.

Then the driver turned on the siren. David punched his fist into the air. Carter's face shone like the polished brass on the fire engine.

Between them, Phoebe clutched her baton tightly.

"We're in the parade!" she said. "All of us. We're in the parade!"

As the sirens blared triumphantly, Phoebe, David, and Carter rode on through town together in Phoebe's parade.